Khmers, Tigers, AND Talismans

FROM THE HISTORY AND LEGENDS OF MYSTERIOUS CAMBODIA

Written by
JEWELL REINHART COBURN

Illustrated by
NENA GRIGORIAN ULLBERG

Research Consultant
SINAL CHAN

Contributors

Blintheuk Samuth
Fany Kim Thiel
Khuon Thongsy

Kong Thann
Leang Hak Chou
Leng Chou Kuon

Men Riem

Also by Jewell Reinhart Coburn

BEYOND THE EAST WIND:
Legends and Folktales of Vietnam

This author holds a Research and Projects grant from the American Association of University Women Educational Foundation.

Text copyright © 1978 Jewell Reinhart Coburn
Illustrations copyright © 1978 Nena Grigorian Ullberg

Burn, Hart and Company Publishers
Thousand Oaks • Box 1772 • California 91360

Library of Congress Cataloging in Publication Data: Coburn, Jewell Reinhart — Khmers, Tigers and Talismans: From the History and Legends of Mysterious Cambodia
SUMMARY: Fictionalized historical account of Jayavarman II, visionary behind the mysterious Cambodian Angkor civilization of 802-1431.
   Includes eight Cambodian legends and folktales: How the Tiger Came to Be, Dak, Kambu and the Seven-Headed Naga, Brave Kong, Neang Kangrei, The Caterpillar and the Crow, Sulayman's Tale of the Maharaja of Zabag, Trial by Ordeal, One of Four. [1. Folklore 2. Cambodia] Ullberg, Nena Gregorian, III.
77-014887
ISBN 0-918060-02-8

Printed in United States of America

DEDICATED

TO THE

CAMBODIAN PEOPLE

AND TO

CAMBODIAN — AMERICAN

FRIENDSHIP

KHMERS, TIGERS, AND TALISMAN'S

From the History and Legends of Mysterious Cambodia

TALES WITHIN THE TALE

A LITTLE EXTRA

Deep in the steaming Cambodian jungle, behind a forbidding, vine covered wall lies the magnificent, mysterious lost city of Angkor Thom. It stands majestic yet deserted at the end of a grand but decaying causeway bordered by terrifying stone creatures.

How did all this come to be? What manner of people lent mind and muscle to achieve such magnificence? Why so vast a city built in so uninhabited a spot?

Who was the genius behind all this?

I

Jaya whirled around. His keen hearing picked up the low, gutteral snarls of a maddened jungle animal.

In a single practiced gesture he swept his fishing net into a tight pack and tucked it into the waist of his sarong.

His back to the river, he assumed a stance of animal wariness. He crouched low.

The jungle shivered.

Then a scream. Not an animal, but a piercing, human cry.

Jaya bolted. Then sprinted in the direction of the cry.

The jungle air clung to him. It was heavy and damp. Thick, moist leaves slapped him as he sped. Green-toned shafts of light sliced the gray air. There was the scent of humus and jungle decay.

His paths were the dim avenues hidden from casual eyes. He recognized each log and low hanging branch. Each pock in the dark jungle floor.

The echoing cry led him in the direction of the clearing near the outcropping rocks and the cave he knew so well.

Then he smelled it. The rank odor of tiger.

The snarls and screams made his flesh crawl.

He crouched behind the protective brush.

What he saw, turned his stomach.

Blood boiled and spurted. It smeared two entangled forms, one animal, one human.

A short-handled knife lay abandoned, useless on the ground. Too far from the human's reach.

Jaya watched, terrified, as the giant tiger lifted the form of a man in his gleaming teeth. High into the air the beast raised him. Then, with a vicious toss of his great head, he flung him free.

The man fell, limp, like a child's rice stalk doll. Dashed against sharp rocks.

Like tropical lightening, the tiger was on him again.

Jaya crouched low behind an uprooted tree trunk.

Coyly, the tiger nudged the stunned body. He rolled it from side to side. Then he sank his teeth deep into the soft flesh at the man's waist. Like a kitten, the beast shook him in gruesome playfulness.

Jaya knew the tiger would soon move in for the kill.

The boy sprang from his place with demonic speed. His ear-splitting cries filled the air. Cries he had heard hunters use when they came through the forests on hunting forays.

They would be his tools now. This was his hunt.

Jaya lurched forward, his movements sharp, stacatto, decisive. Arms shot upward. Forward. Then just as abruptly, he vanished behind another jungle refuge, only to reappear with jagged movements and jagged cries.

Distracted, the tiger glanced up from his prey. The huge beast turned full face to the young, untested hunter. Then Jaya saw it. The livid scar running deep across the beast's skull. The skin lay gaping and torn. The discarded dagger had had its day. But the small knife had been no match for a beast like this. It had only served to heighten his rage.

Jaya played to what he saw. He hurled himself from behind tree trunk to tree trunk. His own dagger glistening in the green jungle sun. He sensed his shrill call reminded the dumb beast of what an able hunter could do.

The tiger paused, erect. Poised, as though weighing in animal terms the taste of blood and flesh against his own immediate survival.

The victim began to writhe.

Seizing the moment, Jaya lunged forward again with the same sharp, threatening movements. Again, the shrill call, now edged with breathlessness.

The tiger stood motionless. For an instant, uncertain.

Then, almost defiantly, the beast spun around.

Jaya lunged again.

The tiger stepped backward. Hesitated. Then he charged from the clearing and back into the green-black of the jungle.

Jaya stood unmoving. He listened for snapping twigs that marked the tiger's retreat. Perhaps to his distant lair, there to nurse his wound. Perhaps to reconsider his own instinctive strategy.

Jaya heard nothing. Only silence. A choking, strangling, silence. Jaya ran to the side of the fallen man whose chest heaved as he fought for breath. Neither of them tried to speak.

Blood coursed from the great clawed gashes. Some seemed to run the full length of the man's body. On his left leg the flesh lay back exposing mottled, fatty tissue.

Beneath lay the ivory white of human bone.

Jaya looked at the man's face twisted in pain. His only utterance, garbled gasps for air.

Jaya knelt to gain a firm hold under the man's shoulders. His grip was insecure. Their bodies were slippery with sweat and blood. Jaya clenched his teeth. His muscles stood out taut and wet. Lifting and dragging, he maneuvered the man in the direction of the cave.

The smell of hot blood hung acrid in the thick air. With his free foot, Jaya attempted to kick the fine dust over the bloody pools.

He strained under the man's weight. Repeatedly, he readjusted his grip. His arms slipped and slid. He felt dizzy from physical exertion in the stiffling heat.

Flashing images darted crazily through his mind. Blood-red images that he could not blink away. Taunting him. Toying with his senses. He remembered red-blood flames. Thick, crimson, firey tongues that devoured homes and consumed villages. Fire that crackled and hissed with fiendish laughter.

As Jaya dragged the man, he felt another heat. Another terror. The screams. The running. Stumbling. Trampling feet. Another human grasp. First, secure. Then, slipping. Loosening. And finally, separation.

That time there had been no hunter's calls. No tricks to deceive that angry assailant, so long ago. No final surge of strength that would reestablish the warmth of hand in hand. That time, wild, dry, eyes of horror. Then loneliness.

Jaya readjusted his grip once more. In an excruciating burst of will, he managed his burden through the opening of the cave and to safety.

There he collapsed, dazed and spent, sprawled on the smooth, cool floor of the cave, beside the stranger's mangled body.

II

"The fact that you outwitted the king of the jungle sobers me, my son," Jaya's new friend, Hiran, told him one day. "The reason I say this is because you know, of course, who is the greatest of all beasts and where he came from?"

"If you say that the tiger is the greatest of all beasts, I know it only because you tell me so. But how the tiger came to be, that I have no way of knowing," replied Jaya. "In fact, I know very little of anything that I can't see directly," Jaya's eyes dropped in embarrassment.

"Ah, my boy, you would humble yourself far too low. You mark this. . ." Hiran waggled a finger in Jaya's direction. "I sense that you are the keeper of knowledge you're unaware of. But of that — another time. Come. Help me closer to the fire. Sit by me and I'll tell you just who it was against whom you proved such an able match."

Jaya pushed the sticks closer together and the small flame danced higher in the warm evening air. The trees stood out white and skeleton-like in the dim twilight. Their gaunt roots entwined as though standing guard before the dense gray jungle fortress.

Someplace beyond, water buffalo plodded their stolid ways homeward. Distant villages blew out their coconut oil candles. Children, spent from play, curled puppy-like and silent on woven floor-mats.

Jaya and Hiran were alone with the jungle whispers. Now and then there was the rustle of leaves. Small, unseen animals going about their night-time chores, Jaya thought. Then the lone call of a night bird winging across dense blue shadows.

Jaya helped Hiran closer to the fire. He noticed that the man gained more strength each day.

His left leg, however, stretched limp, uncooperative.

Hiran watched as Jaya studied his mangled but healing body. "Never mind that leg, son. It will come along at its own pace." He chuckled, resigned. Then his voice softened. "You've been a good boy. Far kinder to a useless fellow than need be."

Hiran thought again of so noble a deed accomplished by so young a boy. He noted again the sturdy frame that made Jaya appear more than the sixteen or seventeen years he must be. He was serene-faced with sensitive, penetrating black eyes.

"And what do I have to pay you for such kindness? Nothing, it would seem, but words, and words, and more. . ."

Jaya broke in. . . "But such stories you tell, my lord. You could go on and on and never stop. I can't get enough. And please. . ." Jaya looked away, then added quietly, "Please don't speak of paying. Fulfilling a duty carries a payment of its own."

12

"Ably said, my son." Hiran beckoned Jaya to sit down beside him. "If you like stories, you will surely like this one."

"It seems, my boy, that this land was once ruled by a king who faced an unsettling dilemma. He called to council the wisest people in his court. First, he summoned his four chief ministers, men of virtue and wisdom, stalwart pillars of his kingdom. He called for the royal astrologer, whose knowledge of celestial matters was always sought in business of gravity. Lastly he summoned his lovely wife.

When everyone was assembled before him, and he knew them to be quite safe from prying eyes and unfriendly ears, he confided, "There are forces abroad in this land that defy ordinary combat. As protector of the realm, I must respond to this threat. But, I am helpless. I am quite unprepared to thwart the influence of evil magic."

The four ministers, the astrologer, and the king's wife sat listening attentively.

"Well, don't just sit there," thundered the king. "Speak up. We have decisions to make. We have a kingdom at stake!"

He turned to the four ministers. "You four. What do you have to say?"

In mumbling unison, the four ministers spoke at once. "Kind Majesty, it would appear that this calls for. . .

. . . further consideration. . ."

". . . time for reflection. . ."

". . . avoid hasty. . ."

"I might have known." and the king, whose ministers he honored more for their deliberate ways than for their speed of thought, scowled.

He looked at the astrologer. "And?" His eyebrows arched in expectation.

13

Never missing a chance to make a favorable impression, the astrologer spoke right up. "Most Gracious King, what is needed here is craft. Cunning. Shrewdness. Cleverness. . ." His words danced a comical jig in the tense air of the royal chambers.

"Yes. Yes. Yes. Yes," interrupted the king. "Look, what I want is a plan of action. Something workable." And the king sat back on this throne, his brow furrowed.

"If His Majesty would be so gracious. . . "

The king looked in the direction of his wife.

"What His Majesty is in need of is extra knowledge. Information to place him in a superior position to his enemies. If it would please His Majesty, His humble wife would recommend that he seek out the wise man from Takkasila. It is said that he is the guardian of mysterious powers."

"Exactly what I was thinking," said the king and, without further comment, announced a pilgrimage.

"Your humble servant suggests," offered the royal wife, "that we plan with care. Take more than enough provisions. Plan for the unexpected."

"Precisely what I was about to say," the king said. "Take enough equipment to see us on an unfamiliar venture."

"And, Your Majesty," his wife spoke again, "it will be well to be accompanied by your closest advisers." The king nodded emphatically. "And each of you, as my wisest counselors, will, of course, accompany me."

The four ministers appeared bewildered at the dazzling speed by which the plans took form.

The astrologer giggled in anticipation.

And the queen begged humble leave to do the work necessary for such an enterprise.

The seven pilgrims hacked their ways through dense underbrush. They scrambled through craggy ravines. In time, they spotted the remote hermitage.

The Wise Man of Takkasila greeted them with sage indifference. He leaned on his gnarled staff and waited to hear the nature of their visit.

The four ministers spoke up first.

"We don't wish to intrude, but . . ."

"It is not our desire to . . ."

"We wouldn't for the world want to. . ."

"It is art. Craft. Skill. Knowledge we want," asserted the astrologer. He stood saber-straight before the bent and wizened hermit.

The king's lovely wife stepped forward politely and said, "We come, Oh, Wise One, seeking enlightenment. The enemy of our kingdom has evil powers. We ask that you teach us ways to overcome those powers so that peace might return to our realm."

The king stepped forward proudly. "That was just what I was going to say."

"I understand," was the wise man's only reply.

The next day, instruction began in earnest. The hermit taught wonderful and mysterious incantations. Charms. Magic brews. Sorcery of every kind imaginable.

The day arrived when the lessons were over.

The royal party bade farewell to the wise man and set out for home.

But they had not traveled far, when they were beset with a series of mishaps. First, they lost their way. Next, the king stepped on a thorn. And then the astrologer forgot what day it was.

There, in the middle of the jungle, the king called a council. "So, now what do we do?" he asked imperiously.

The chief ministers suggested they weigh the situation.

15

The astrologer said he would need to work up new calculations.

It was the royal wife who suggested they use some of the lessons learned from the wise man.

"Those were my very thoughts," said the king.

"If it pleases His Lordship, we could change ourselves into a creature who can survive in this jungle," offered his wife.

The king was elated. "We must be lithe and beautiful. Here, Wife, stand behind me."

"We must be deliberate and powerful. You four." He waved toward the ministers. "Line up behind my royal wife."

The astrologer scampered to his place behind the ministers. "We must be cunning, crafty, shrewd, and clever," he said.

Then, together, they all said,

"Som-botho-sak-sith-teang-lay-mok-chuop-chom-knea-
samdeng-nov-pheap-dar-aschar-muoy!"*

The earth shook. The sky shivered. Trees swayed and boulders crashed in thunderous avalanches.

When quiet was finally restored, there, in the jungle clearing, stood a beast of magnificent proportions. His legs, sturdy and powerful, strong, like four mighty pillars of some great kingdom. The tail waved smartly as though it had a wisdom of its own. When it moved, the beast's body was supple and graceful like that of a beautiful queen. And its head? Ah, greater, more majestic, than any had ever seen.

And for the finishing touch, stripes encircled its body. Black enamel on gold.

---

* Cambodian for, "May all forces, both natural and supernatural, work together for our cause!"

"Since that time, Jaya, the tiger has been the king of all beasts. And why not, when you consider how he came to be."

The two chuckled. Jaya stretched.

"Are you tired, my boy? Should we call it a night?"

"As you say," said Jaya.

"I'm not really ready for sleep. How about one last story while the fire burns low?"

"I would like that."

"So it shall be." Hiran shifted his position in a fruitless effort to find comfort and ease the pain. "For an ending, I will tell of beginnings. How would that be, Jaya? I will tell you what was told to me a long, long time ago. About the people in this beautiful land. Who they were. Where they came from. What they were like, so long ago."

Jaya leaned forward, his head on his hand.

Hiran began . . .

"Some two thousand years ago, Dak, The Forest Dweller, came down to the big river. He had made suitable prayers to the Great Cobra, father of all creation. Now Dak had had a dream. There came to him information that things were not going to remain as they had been in the great forest for these hundreds of years.

Dak worried about this dream. He had been comfortable with palm-leaf roof and rough teak floor, and rain that fell occasionally. True, tigers and elephants caused trouble more often than he cared to think about. But then, there were always berries to be found in the shadowy marshes.

Basically, he had few problems, save an occasional bush war.

Now according to the dream, Dak was to plant a kind of grain in the mud of the river land. He was to give up war, and hunting, and fishing, while he sat quietly and watched what magic might develop.

Dak had some misgivings about the success of such a venture but one does not go contrary to the wishes of the serpents that control human destiny.

Now in the same night of early time, one Kambu, a young Indian nobleman slept the sleep of one drugged with the fragrance of the Samanea flower. The tropical heat pressed close around him. It held him in breathless bondage.

As though out of a dream, Kambu suddenly sensed a presence — an eerie, indistinct presence.

A flash of terror ripped through him. He tried to move but could not. He writhed inwardly, and tried vainly to open his eyes. But, he could not.

Then he heard it.

A faint whisper, "Tomorrow. . . tomorrow. . ."

The young Indian adventurer wrestled with sleep.

"Tomorrow. . ." He heard it again.

Kambu strained.

"Tomorrow, you will depart from this place and travel East. . ."

The sound undulated as though floating on a thick, inky sea.

"Eastward, you will travel. . . Eastward, you will sail . . ."

Closer. Clearer now.

". . . and you will take with you the cross bow and the quiver of arrows invested with divine powers. . . and Dak, the sorcerer. . . You will take with you this man of magic."

Kambu's mind reeled. "I have no magic cross bow and arrows," he wanted to shout. "And who is this Dak?"

20

"Tomorrow. . . tomorrow. . ." The whisper faded into the distant rustle of the window hangings. Shortly, Kambu again slept heavily.

The morning dawned blinding and brilliant. The hot tropical sun unloosed the bonds of sleep. Kambu awoke with a start. As though charged with a single thought, he rose, dressed, and faced the eastern sun.

He paused, puzzled. "What am I doing?" Then as though nudged by a distant memory, he recalled the incident of the night before.

"Wait a minute," he cautioned himself. "Dreams are hardly marching orders," and he determined to take this matter to the temple to seek out some wise man who could interpret his dream.

He dressed hurriedly and made his way to the temple. As he ran across its courtyard, he stopped abruptly. There by a pillar lay a cross bow with a quiver of arrows. He approached it cautiously. He saw that it was no ordinary bow but rather one that by its intricacy of design compelled him to pick it up. To examine it more closely. He took the bow into his hand, raised it to his chest amazed that it seemed hewn and fashioned for him alone.

Its shank fit exactly the length of his arm. His hand felt comfortable with the bow in its grasp.

Kambu slung the quiver strap over his shoulder and it positioned itself precisely to the contour of his shoulders and back.

This, he decided, was the interpretation he sought. "But what of the sorcerer, Dak?" Kambu mused recalling further details of the dream.

Leaving the question unanswered, Kambu set his sights eastward, toward the morning sun.

He traveled early, reserving the stifling afternoon heat and the oppressive nights to renew his strength. Over treacherous mountain ridges he traveled. Across vast lowlands and fertile valleys until he came to a majestic river stretching before him.

At this juncture the sorcerer, Dak, looked up from his work. Standing before him he saw a weary-faced young man whose skin, instead of being bared to the sun as the gods had intended it be, was encased in layer upon layer of cloth. In his hand he carried a cross bow.

"Who are you?" asked Dak.

"My name is Kambu," replied the stranger. I am Prince of Arya Deca, and Siva, the great god, is my father-in-law."

Dak raised his hand. "The great god is not Siva," he said. "It is the king of Nagas whose name I shouldn't dare to repeat even if I remembered it."

Kambu wasn't impressed. He stared at the bit of grain in Dak's hand.

"What have you there?"

"Magic. I was instructed in a dream to bring this to the bank of the great river and to plant it. I've squatted on my heels for several rounds of the moon. I'm beginning to question the whole project. Maybe I should throw it away."

"Oh, no!" Kambu cried. "Here is more potent magic than you suspect. All the world about is sere and desert. In my own land, hot winds have withered everything. When I look at this magic you have I can look into the future. I see a great nation growing here in this valley."

"Am I to understand that you, an adventurer, have greater understanding of this magic than I, a sorcerer?"

"No offense intended," Kambu answered.

"I don't understand."

"You will. Here, help me lash these logs together. We will make a craft that can withstand any of the whims of the water gods."

Suddenly Dak remembered the rest of his dream. He was to lead some prince to the court of Serpents and by so doing, would one day be a great chief himself.

But the thought of entering the kingdom of Nagas slowed him somewhat. He had heard terrifying stories of the great crystal caverns inhabited by the seven-headed serpents.

Nonetheless, he helped Kambu lash the logs together and together they pushed their craft away from the shore.

The eastern sun beckoned them out into the surf and into the vast watery plains.

No sooner had they lost sight of land than a great wind surged about them. It buffeted and tossed them playfully. Their paddles no longer steered them. The canoe dipped and bobbed crazily on a course all its own.

Kambu lashed his paddle to the gunwales of the vessel. He strapped the magic crossbow to himself and crouched low in the canoe. Then, he and Dak surrendered themselves to nature.

Kambu knew what it was to be a servant to nature. Already he had been driven across the Bay of Bengal, and through the Malaccan Straits. He was blown around the peninsula now known as Singapore. Up the South China Sea and to the coast of Indo-China where this story began.

And, as before, as abruptly as it began, the winds stopped. Kambu and Dak were left in mirrored silence. As they strained to see ahead of them, their spirits suddenly rose. Stretching before them lay a ribbon of land, an emerald strip against an azure sea.

Kambu unlashed his paddle and headed toward the shore. He looked back over his shoulder and saw the vast waters fading into the morning haze. He turned again to the land. But there, a canoe, streamlined, graceful as a water serpent, suddenly materialized and sped toward them.

"Strange that I did not see the canoe before," Kambu thought.

Like an arrow the canoe stayed on course. Kambu swung his craft to the left. The speeding canoe did likewise. He turned deftly to the right. The slender canoe did the same.

Spellbound, Kambu studied the fast moving vessel. He noted its stately lines, its exquisitely carved helm. When it came close enough for him to see the crew, he was shocked to find a maiden maneuvering the craft like a seasoned seaman. Kambu had never seen greater beauty before.

23

Kambu smiled broadly and, lifting his hands together, bowed his head slightly in the formal greeting used by Southeast Asians since time began. He lowered his eyes with respect and friendliness. Dak did likewise.

In response, Kambu felt a slap of hot air against his cheek and heard the zing of an arrow past his ear.

In fear, Dak wedged himself under the seat of the canoe.

Kambu instinctively snatched his cross bow and returned the greeting. His arrow came to rest at the maiden's feet.

Unsmiling, the girl glared at him. She leaned down to pick up the arrow and return it from her own bow but it resisted her grasp. She tried again and again but it would not yield.

"Is this any way to greet two tired, lost seamen?" called Kambu to the maiden.

She glowered at them and reached into her own quiver for a fresh arrow. She pulled at it but it resisted her touch. She fingered another arrow. It too held firm.

"You are invading my waters," she accused. Her angry words melted into the sound of a child's song as they rose and fell with the surf.

"I have not come to invade your land," Kambu told her.

"Then you are trespassing. Uninvited. Unwanted." And she once again yanked at the arrows behind her.

"You misunderstand."

"I misunderstand nothing." her beautiful eyes flashed with anger. "Release my arrows," she demanded.

Kambu chuckled, as much at the maiden, as at the magic of the cross bow. "I release your arrows? In your state of mind?"

"I'll not stand for this," she cried.

"And what will you do if I withhold my magic?"

"You'll see." With new strength she pulled free one of her arrows. With a flash like sun against a fish's iridescent tail, she hurled it straight toward Kambu's heart.

But Kambu's magic arrow caught it in mid-flight. It snapped, then fell in a spray of splinters into the water.

"Don't think for a minute that I haven't dealt with intruders like you," she shouted. "Many like you lie dead on the bottom of this river. You're no different. You'll not put the prow of your canoe on the shores of my land."

Without further words Kambu pulled another arrow from the magic quiver. This one he let fly at the stern of the maiden's craft. Her canoe spun about. As it came full turn, Kambu fired again. This time at the bow. The canoe turned again. He fired again and again and the maiden's canoe spun faster and faster. She too fired arrow after arrow but her turning boat confused her aim.

Her last arrow fired, she cried, "What would you have of me?"

Laughing at the cowed but lovely maiden, Kambu stopped his barrage of arrows. Dak peeked over the gunwale.

When the two crafts came to a standstill, Kambu looked deep into the lovely face of his attacker and replied, "Nothing but to be your friend and to be guided to the great king of the Nagas."

"Never!" she hissed.

So Kambu reached into his quiver and drew out his last arrow. In a single shot, it pierced her canoe broadside. The hole gaped and gasped with great swallows of sea water. The maiden's canoe tottered and heaved crazily. Listing to the side, it slipped forlornly beneath the water's surface. When the maiden cried for help, Kambu reached across Dak and lifted her gently into his canoe.

"I would let nothing happen to you."

The girl wavered for an instant, her hostility untwisting into a look of awe. "No one has outmaneuvered the Naga Princess, daughter of the ruler of this realm," she finally managed. "How is it that you have such powers?"

"No doubt because I come only in friendship." Having spoken, Kambu took from a cask tucked in the back of his canoe Indian silks as shimmering as the eastern sun that danced across the morning ripples. He pulled out jewels and ivory. These he laid before the beautiful princess.

"Come, I will take you to my father, the King of all Snakes," she consented.

Dak cowered at the entrance to the great crystal throne room, but Kambu faced the King Cobra unafraid. In a loud voice that reverberated throughout the great crystal hall, he cried, "I am Prince Kambu from the land of Arya Deca. Princess Mera, the beautiful foster daughter of the god Siva, was once my wife. But Siva, in a rage, destroyed the crops, and my people died of hunger. Siva took back my wife, Mera, and, alone in a desolate country, my grief overwhelmed me. So I left." He paused briefly, then continued, "I traveled across great waters, across mountains and vast deserts until I came to the great river that flows by your kingdom. I met the sorcerer Dak who gave me magic in the form of rice. If it is your will that I settle here, I will make use of the rice kernels to raise up a nation of servants to the high gods. If not, then kill me for I can go no further."

For some days the king of Nagas thought about Kambu's proposal. His daughter had, in the meantime, fallen in love with the handsome stranger. She pleaded with her father to spare his life and allow him to remain in the land.

Now, as our grandfathers tell us, the Naga Princess was actually another of the seven-headed serpents, graceful, protecting, providing spirits of the water.

After she married the brave Indian adventurer, Master of the Land, she gave birth to the beautiful people who became known as Kambujas, or, children of Kambu.*

*In time, the name was changed to Cambodge, and still later, Cambodia.
The dynasty of Kambu and the Naga Princess is said to have lasted a mythical one-hundred and fifty generations.

26

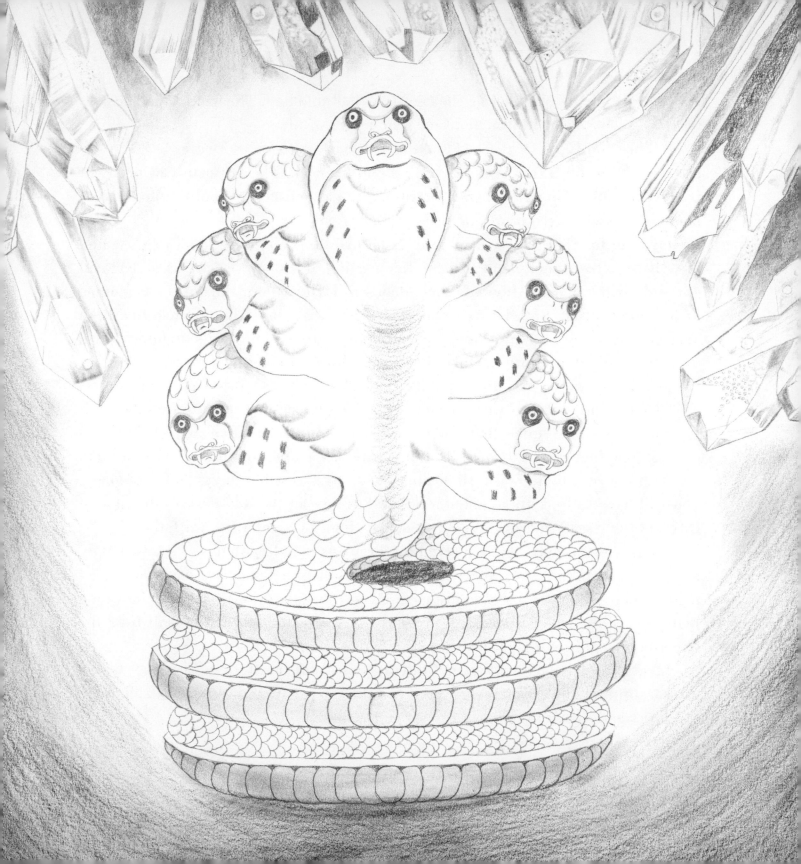

Jaya sat silently, pondering the tale Hiran had told him. The night fire danced as night fires have danced throughout the generations of time.

Unconsciously, Jaya reached for the talisman that, for as long as he could remember, hung on a thin strip of reed around his neck. The talisman had been cut from Cambodia's finest pink-gray sandstone. It was polished. Smooth. Like the rose marble reserved for sculptures of highest quality.

Jaya ran his finger over its surface, as he had done countless times in his young life. His sensitive touch identified the fine carving of a single letter — complete and graceful, in the dancing flow of Cambodian script. He could make out the beginning of a second letter. But the final, deciding swirl, was gone. The talisman had been damaged. Jaya did not know how. He could remember nothing of its origin. Nothing of its fragmented inscription. Only, that he had always worn it.

For many moments Hiran watched the boy. Finally, he broke the silence.

"That stone that you wear at your neck. I have seen that it bears a symbol. But my son, I have also noted that it is an imperfect symbol. One that suggests but does not tell, one that speaks, but says nothing. It points a direction, but no destination."

With concern in his voice, Hiran continued, "It is possible, Jaya, that, like many, you will have to look to a common origin. Possibly all the way back to the time of Dak and the Naga Princess. You may, one day, look to Kambu as your father."

"But, about one thing, I am certain," Hiran asserted, brightening. "I have watched you through the rising and falling of many suns since our lives have touched. I believe there will come a season just as surely as the seasons of dryness and monsoon that you will be called great. But, my child, your greatness will not result from the imperfect inscription that you wear around your neck."

Jaya looked long into the fire, but not once did he unloose his grasp of the carved stone at his throat. Nor would his mind expel those mysterious, splintered memories and shards of images from his past.

III

"Don't move. Face the fire and don't turn around."
The voice was crude and demanding yet youthful — the
voice of someone about Jaya's own age.

Jaya did as he was told. His throat tightened.

Hiran must have stirred inside the cave. Jaya sensed
the attention diverted.

"You in the cave," the same voice demanded. "Hold
it!" The youth turned back to Jaya. "How many are in
there?"

Before Jaya could answer, the voice commanded,
"Tell them we spare no one who defies us. Why waste a
worthless jungle insect."

Jaya sat silent and rigid. The fish he was roasting
spat and sizzled on the stick over the fire. He heard

nothing more from the cave.

Suddenly he was surrounded. Through menacing, pointed sticks, Jaya stared into the faces of a ragged band of boys, dirty and haggard.

"I said, who is in there?" This time the speaker stood over Jaya. Lean and wild looking, slightly shorter than Jaya, he wore only a frayed, filthy loin cloth.

"When Prithivin gives an order, he gets action." His voice was surly and his upper lip rolled back exposing teeth yellowed from lack of care and proper nutrition.

The leader stepped stealthily backward, keeping his eye on Jaya. He motioned for the others to close in around him. Then he spun about to look into the cave opening.

Prithivin peered into the blackness and called, "You, in there. Get out here and bring everything of value you have."

Jaya summoned his courage. "He cannot come out on his own."

"I didn't ask you," the leader shot back over his shoulder. Then he shouted again, "You, in there. Out!"

There was no movement. No response.

"I guess you didn't hear me. This is Prithivin."

"I assure you that if he were able, he would," offered Jaya.

Prithivin held his ground at the cave's opening.

"Ah, so there is only one in there. Then if he won't come, you get him out here;" Prithivin demanded and menacingly pointed his lance at Jaya.

Jaya stood up. As he turned, he felt the sharp tips of the boys' prodding weapons on his back. Unresisting, Jaya moved to the entrance of the cave. The boys took position behind him. Jaya entered the darkness and went directly to Hiran's mat. "Five of them," he whispered.

"Obey them," was Hiran's only replay.

"Out now!" The leader shouted from the entrance.

Jaya helped Hiran onto his one strong leg, supporting him the best he could.

They made their way to the opening of the cave. When the boys saw the cripple leaning heavily on Jaya, they jeered and howled.

"Those two aren't worth our bother," one of the boys sneered.

"I don't call this much of a catch," hissed another.

"Look here. We're out for bigger things. If you'd listened to me. . ."

"Cripples aren't fair game." They turned away grumbling.

Jaya noticed that none of the boys appeared to be more than sixteen, the age Jaya judged himself to be. One of the band seemed very much younger than the others. Jaya noticed he handled his lance awkwardly. He seemed to hang back from the others. His comments were lost in the others' noisy scorning.

The boys' curiosity satisfied, their interest shifted abruptly. Once convinced that Hiran and Jaya posed no threat, they turned to a matter of keener interest.

"We'll take those." Prithivin swaggered forward and grabbed at the delicious smelling fish. "What else you got there?" He didn't wait for an answer. "Whatever it is, it's ours."

The boys moved in on the fish. "Stand back," Prithivin ordered. "What's that rolled in the leaf? Rice? Give it here."

"There is only enough for two," managed Jaya.

"Doesn't matter." The leader shrugged and turned back to the fire.

The others clamored to their leader's side. "Back, back," he ordered.

Hiran stepped forward. "Here, my sons," he said, producing from under his tunic dried fish and a large leaf of rice left from the previous day's meal, "add this to your meal. What there is by the fire can't possibly satisfy all of you."

He handed the food to Jaya who held it out to the boys. The leader snatched it from him and laid it out next to the freshly cooked food by the fire. The boys turned to Hiran. For a moment, they looked confused. Then, in a flury of motion, they were fumbling and groping in their tunics. By the fire, appeared another rolled leaf. Then another. And yet another. Before the twilight crept away, there lay a

31

feast before the band of miserable, starved boys. A banquet of dirty, shapeless wads of stolen meat, and fish, and gray-white rice.

"And so it is to Siva, the great protector and provider that each of us can be thankful for all this," Hiran told them as he and Jaya watched while the ragged boys ripped and tore at the food before them.

Blanketed by the jungle night and gentled by filled bellies, the boys gradually grew jovial and talkative. Soon they chattered like the gibbons that swing playfully from limb to limb.

Jaya and Hiran learned that the band of ruffians had been in the jungles for months. Sometimes lost. Sometimes happening upon villages of unsuspecting victims. They were rootless. Restless. United by a pathetic allegiance to an impossible dream. A dream of riches, if worthless baubles can be called wealth. And food. Begged and stolen from victims poorer yet than they.

Jaya and Hiran sat on a log not far from the fire. While the ragged boys tussled each other like playful cubs, Prithivin broke away unnoticed. He sidled to the end of the log and spoke to Jaya in low tones.

"Been out here all your life?"

"Not exactly all," Jaya replied touching the stone at his neck.

"This man your father?"

"No," Jaya answered.

"Then what are you doing out here with him? A relative?"

"No." Jaya hesitated, then he said, "I don't think Hiran can live out here alone."

"Does it matter? We've learned to survive. All of us lived in the village once. Forget him."

"That wouldn't be so easy."

"What do you mean?"

"He's my friend."

"Friend? You're joking. I say if a friend can't do you any good, what good is a friend?"

"But he does good."

"Yeh, good like lift me up. Set me down. Feed me. That's good?"

"No, not that. I mean good in other ways."

"What other way is there?"

"Well, he teaches me."

Prithivin spat with disdain. "Look, if it's lessons you want, I'm the one to teach them. See those guys over there? Not a one of them knew straight up until I came along. I taught them every trick they know. And I've hardly begun. Give us a little time and we'll have every villager shaking when they hear the name Prithivin. When they hear I'm on my way, they will run out of their huts and beg to heap their gold at my feet."

You live in the jungle now?" asked Jaya.

"Right."

"You know the jungle well?"

"Of course."

"Oh."

"What do you mean, 'oh'?"

"Just some things I noticed."

"Like?"

"Remember how your boys ate? They never looked up from the food. Animals can smell good food too, you know."

"Are you saying we don't know the ways of the jungle?"

"I only mentioned this one careless act."

Suddenly Prithivin's voice was loud and bullying, as it had been when he first encountered Jaya and Hiran. He leaned close to Jaya.

"Nobody knows the jungle better than I do. Or my boys." Prithivin took a sharp stone and began filing the hideous barb on his thin lance.

Jaya cringed.

At this, Hiran leaned close. In a half-whisper, he said to Prithivin, "I couldn't help over-hearing what you said. I'm sure Jaya meant only that the jungles are harsh playgrounds."

"So? Nobody tells Prithivin anything," and he was on his feet. Defiantly, he strutted away toward his comrades. His fist tightened and retightened around his weapon. The muscles on his forearm stood out taut and sinewy.

A shiver ran across Jaya's shoulders and down his back.

IV

Jaya was on his feet. He seemed to be the first to hear the cry.

The others stirred, sluggish with sleep. By the time they were dimly aware, Jaya was already out of sight. He leaped fallen logs and ran in the direction of the great river that flowed beyond the tiny jungle clearing.

He could hear it more distinctly now. The panting, half-cries of one in serious danger.

He spread the thick foliage at the water's edge. His stomach muscles tightened.

"Prithivin!" Jaya saw the boy's body held fast by the tendrils and vines of the water plants at the river's edge. His legs dangled beneath the surface.

"I can't move," gasped Prithivin. "He's coming at

me." Prithivin's eyes flashed terror Jaya understood well.

Then Jaya saw it. The huge menacing green-brown body barely broke the water's surface. It made its grim way directly toward Prithivin.

"Pull yourself up. Get your legs out of the water," Jaya yelled.

"I can't. I can't move."

With lightning speed, Jaya wrapped his arms around Prithivin's waist and heaved him feet first up onto the fern and vine-covered bank. Prithivin cried out in pain.

The giant head surfaced. The enraged crocodile swam dead-on toward the boy.

Jaya's dagger hacked away the vines. "Run!" Jaya commanded.

Prithivin did not move.

"Run, I tell you. Get out of here!"

"I can't. I can't move!"

The great crocodile reached the shore. Enraged at the prospect of losing its victim, it pulled its body from the water in determined pursuit.

On land its movements slowed. Without the help of the buoyant water, the creature heaved his lumbering body into the hot air.

Jaya reached down and hoisted Prithivin onto his shoulders. Staggering under his weight, he carried him like a trussed animal away from his pursuer.

Near the clearing, they were met by the shouts of the boys. Calling, they ran toward them and helped Jaya carry Prithivin back to the cave. There they laid him on Hiran's mat.

"It's my back. I can't move, I tell you," and Jaya noticed tears welling in the eyes of the once boastful Prithivin.

The days passed and Prithivin was slow to recover.

The other four boys assumed a sort of routine, passing the time waiting for their leader. They learned from Jaya when to hunt and where to fish. They learned to detect an approaching animal, where to take refuge.

One night they huddled, forlorn and leaderless near the cave opening not far from the protective fire. Hiran hobbled toward the little group and sat with them. Jaya helped Prithivin to the circle and in the quiet before sleep claims its children, Hiran told them the very old story of another boastful young fellow — one known as Brave Kong.

"Now Kong also led a small band of adventurers. His band consisted of his two wives. One's name was Ahm. The other, Kum.

Early one day the three of them set off to visit Kong's elder brother who lived in a far village beyond the jungle.

They walked along the quiet, shaded, path that meandered through the forest. They marveled at the delicate ferns, their leaves like green lace. Palm fronds arched gracefully from smooth, stately tree trunks. Miniature blossoms perched on thread-like stems. A sweet fragrance filled the air.

Suddenly, an abrasive, sand-papery growl and the angry, raspy breathing of some terrible beast invaded the quiet beauty.

In a flash, Kong darted to the safety of a hollow tree trunk. In that same flash, a tiger stepped from the thicket and stood before the two wives. The two women seized pieces of falling limbs. Using them as clubs, they beat the poor tiger senseless.

The wives' decisive action and forthright manner caught the beast unaware and before you could count, "mouy, pee, bay," the tiger lay lifeless at their feet.

Kong peered from the safety of the tree trunk. When he saw the great tiger subdued he ran from hiding. He scurried about this way and that. Finally he picked up one of the limbs and began clubbing the dead animal.

"And what is all this supposed to mean," asked Ahm, her bare foot tapping the ground indignantly.

"And what kind of lily-livered man comes to beat a tiger somebody else has killed?" demanded Kum.

Kong did not answer but continued beating the dead carcass. When he had satisfied himself, he tied the tiger's legs together with vines. He slung the great body between two poles. Then he placed the poles on the shoulders of his two wives.

He set off again, leading Ahm and Kum, muttering loudly, "Nonsense. There isn't a woman in the world who could beat a tiger to death."

When they emerged from the jungle into the village clearing, the townspeople saw them and began shouting. "Come and see! Here is a man who must be very brave! This tiger has been menacing us for years. Tell us, brave Sir, how did you do this?"

Kong ordered his wives to take the poles from their shoulders. The lifeless hulk fell to the ground. Kong put a foot up on it, his hands on his hips.

"It is all very simple," he boasted. "When the tiger rushed me, I merely met him like this . . ." Kong exchanged his stance for that of a Cambodian boxer. His fists raised.

His description was indeed impressive. So impressive, that it won him a new name. From then on, he was known as Brave Kong, the man who boxes tigers.

Word of Kong's feat reached royal ears. Kong was promptly summoned. The king was forever looking for brave men. He declared Kong a royal officer.

Kong enjoyed his reputation completely. He reenacted the jungle encounter for anyone who would listen.

So, it was most natural that Brave Kong was chosen when the king learned that his land was about to be invaded.

Kong felt suddenly weak inside. He ran home and cowered in the corner of his hut.

"Come. Come, now" his wives encouraged. "What you have been commanded to do, you must do."

"But what do I know about armies?" wailed Kong.

"A good meal will lift your spirits."

"Food?" he replied wanly.

Finally, nothing would do but Ahm and Kum, one on each side, marched Kong off to battle.

He was hoisted onto the back of a great warrior elephant and directed to the head of the king's army.

For a time he traveled uneventfully astride the lumbering beast.

But Kong's fright began to get the best of him. First his hands began to tremble. Then his arms and shoulders began to shake.

Finally Kong was shaking so violently that his legs knocked against the elephant's head.

His elephant had been finely trained. Responding obediently to what he took to be Kong's signal to advance, the elephant broadened his stride and took off in a full run.

The whole royal army followed in hot pursuit.

In a frenzy of cowardice, the opposing forces broke rank and scattered.

Seeing the enemy routed, Kong raised his arm in victory.

"Brave Sir," dared a corporal. "I submit that your victory came from fear. My men tell me they saw you trembling."

"Trembling, yes," shouted the triumphant Kong. "Trembling with excitement!"

And the soldiers had no choice but to accept his explanation. Kong out-ranked and out-talked them all.

Kong came away from the palace heaped yet higher with honors and awards, gifts from a grateful king.

General Kong was nearing the climax of one of his extravagant tales one day, when the king's courier came upon him. Seeing him, Kong winced.

"What did you do then?" the enraptured crowd pressed him.

"Try to imagine," he said hastily and attempted to sneak away unnoticed.

But the crowd would not have that. Kong had no choice but to stand his ground. Meekly, he followed the courier back to the king once more.

This time he was assigned the task of destroying a great crocodile who had menaced the people for years.

"This time will surely be my last," Kong moaned to his wives. "What do I know about crocodiles?"

"Well, you can't tell that to the king," said Ahm and Kum. And Brave Kong moaned all the more.

"I know what I'll do," he said woefully. "I'll just jump in the water in front of the crocodile and have it over with."

His wives patted his shoulder understandingly.

People gathered along the river bank for the spectacle. Kong groaned inside. He walked to the edge of the water. The fearsome crocodile lay asleep. Hanging down over the water's surface were the gnarled roots of a gigantic banyon tree. Kong stood trembling in indecision. Then he closed his eyes. Thinking this would surely be his end, he took a gasp of air and leaped into the water.

Kong was no swimmer. He landed with an awful splash and sank like a boulder.

Unbeknown to him, the noise caused by his splash so startled the sleeping crocodile that it reared up in fright only to lodge his great head in the fork of the over hanging tree roots.

When Kong finally surfaced dizzily, he spied the hopelessly entangled crocodile.

With that, Kong reached up. He broke off a protruding branch. Using it as a lance, he drove it through the terror-stricken crocodile.

Everyone on the bank shouted their praises."

The four boys laughed heartily at the tale. They playfully pushed and punched each other.

Jaya sensed the story had a different point for each.

Prithivin merely stared into the fire.

V

The night fire snapped and spat. The stoking log finally gave way. It broke in two in a spray of orange-red embers. Jaya stirred.

He looked over at Hiran who was sleeping heavily, exhausted from the burden of willing his uncooperative limbs to accomplish simple daily tasks.

Prithivin lay unmoving some distance from his brothers in crime. For the time, he was free of pain. The others lay in a haphazard heap to one side of the cave entrance. Jaya recalled that they had never slept so close to the opening.

Mechanically, he got up from his mat to replenish the fire. He made his way around the sleeping bodies, through the opening of protective rocks toward the dying fire. Suddenly, he was aware of a presence.

A hand touched his shoulder lightly.

"Jaya," a hushed voice whispered. "Follow me." The form crept soundlessly ahead of Jaya.

It was Kavindra.

Kavindra, the youngest of the band, seemed a most unlikely conspirator in crime. He did not look back to see if Jaya was following. He seemed confident that his summons was obeyed.

"What is this," managed Jaya still somewhat dazed with sleep.

"I must talk to you."

Jaya protested. "There isn't much night left. We have work ahead of us. There is food to gather, and firewood. Besides, it's dangerous so far from the cave."

"You won't need so much food tomorrow," Kavindra told him. "Only enough for three."

"Three?" Jaya asked, puzzled.

"I will talk fast before Surya and the others notice I'm not with them and ready for the break."

"The break?"

"This morning. Just before sunup."

"But Prithivin can't keep up with you. Where are you going?" Suddenly wary, "You don't know the jungle well enough to travel by dark."

"That's why they are leaving just before daybreak. Surya thinks he knows these trails well enough for an hour's hike without light. When the sun comes up, we will be well on our way."

"And Prithivin?" Jaya persisted.

"What about Prithivin? Surya is taking over from now on. They will do what he says."

"Surya! He knows even less than Prithivin about the jungle. But what about you? Why are you telling me all this anyway?"

44

"I must tell you." Kavindra's voice seemed suddenly younger than usual. He couldn't be much more than a child. Jaya felt him small and frightened sitting by his side on the cold boulder. Kavindra had never been arrogant and boastful like the others. He seemed somehow different.

"Jaya," he whispered. And then Jaya felt it. The wispy touch of hair, long hair, against his arm, "Jaya, I'm not Surya's brother. I'm not Kavindra. My real name is Laksmei. I'm Surya's sister."

Jaya whistled softly.

"I'm forced to go with him and his insane plans."

Jaya felt a surge of gentleness, then defiance. So this is why Kavindra had seemed different from the others. "No one has to do what he feels is not right," Jaya declared.

Resigned, she said, "I do."

"What are you doing traveling with this band of cut-throats anyway?" demanded Jaya.

"Surya is my only living relative. Our mother and father are both dead. And our grandparents are gone too. There are only Surya and me."

"And you agree to them abandoning Prithivin?"

"I have no choice. Anyway, Prithivin himself taught us that. I guess he'll live to regret his own cruel lesson. They figure he's useless now. Only you seem to know what good a cripple can be."

Jaya worked a small hole in the dusty earth with his toe. "So Surya thinks now is the time for the get away without Prithivin to hold you back." He ran his foot back and forth over the shallow depression. "Why did you tell me this?"

"Because I've watched the way you care for Hiran, so crippled and helpless. And I saw how you helped the savage Prithivin even though you must have known he'd turn on you if he felt reason to. You teach even your enemies how to hunt and fish, how to survive in this place."

For a time Jaya and Laksmei sat in silence. The occasional cry of a bird and the movement of leaves wove a thin tissue of sound around them. Here and there the moon pushed through the trees and shimmered momentarily in spangles of light.

"I respect you, Jaya. I wanted you to know."

"But if you feel so strongly, I still don't understand why you follow them."

"Let me explain it this way, Jaya. The way Hiran explains things to you and to Prithivin when you are sitting together near the fire.

Before my mother died she told me many stories. Stories much like Hiran tells you. I'm going to tell you one of those. It's a story filled with horror, just like my own life with these cruel boys. But it is also a story of truth. A truth I cannot deny."

Laksmei huddled close to Jaya to ward off the night chill. Then she began . . .

"There lived a mighty king who, after he had married a very beautiful young maiden, learned that she had eleven other sisters. Wishing to show his sense of duty toward his wife's family, the king summoned her sisters to the palace, married them and gave comfortable quarters to each one.

One day when the king left the palace on a hunting spree in the forests, the Spirit of the Woods saw him. What she saw pleased her. Immediately she determined that she would have the king as a husband. So she changed herself into the most beautiful and alluring of temptresses. When the king came to a clearing, he knelt down to take a drink from the sparkling waters of a cool spring. When he looked up, he saw the woman bathing. She wove about him such a magic spell the king succumbed to her power. According to her plan, he fell desperately in love with her.

The king decided nothing would do but to take the woman back to his palace

and marry her, too. Now the Woods Spirit felt triumphant. She basked in the glory of her accomplishment. . . until she learned the king already had twelve wives.

"This, I will not tolerate," she told herself. "I will secure the help of an astrologer.

Artfully she bribed him. She told him to make up a story the king would believe. After all, the king had faith in the astrologer before.

In due time the shifty astrologer informed the king that his twelve wives were each about to give birth to a boy child. But, he hastened to add, this would be no occasion to celebrate. Each of the infants would be cursed with ill health. A shame to the throne. . .

Gloom descended upon the royal household. So melancholy did the king become that his new wife soothed him by offering to resolve the situation herself.

The miserable king consented.

Now unbeknown to anyone, the evil queen had already laid a plan. Her plan was that none of the twelve wives would annoy the king again.

She ordered the chief minister to assign each wife to live out her life at the dark bottom of a waterless well.

Shocked, the minister asked, "But, my great Queen, is such a destiny warranted? It is so dark and chilly in the well."

"Darkness will be of no concern to them," she snapped.

"How so?" he asked.

"You need only to follow my orders. Listen with care. First, you will pluck out their eyes. Then you will bring the eyes to me in this." She thrust a large, round jar at him.

The minister gasped.

Nevertheless he was compelled to obey her command.

And so it happened that each of the blinded wives did give birth to a boy child. True to the evil prediction, each infant became ill and died. That is, all but the infant son of the youngest wife.

Under his blind mother's tender care, the son grew to fine manhood. One day, he escaped from the well.

The young man's fine and honorable reputation soon caught the attention of the evil queen. With her crafty insight, she suspected his identity. She ordered him followed. When it was reported that he was seen to lower food into the waterless well each day, the evil queen's suspicions were confirmed.

"Bring that young man to me," she ordered.

When he stood before her, she said, "Because I have heard fine reports of you, I wish you to carry out a mission for me. I believe you, and you alone, are suitable for it," she said, flattering him.

"Gladly would I serve my queen," he agreed.

He knew, of course, that he had no choice.

"A life of ease and comfort will be yours if you deliver this important message to my daughter in a far country."

"And, if I do this for you, my Gracious Queen, you will feed the twelve women in the well during my absence?"

The evil queen agreed — actually this time she had no choice.

So the fine young man set about his mission. He carried the message in a cylinder strapped across his shoulder.

One night while he slept weary from his long journey, a wondering ascetic happened by.

When he stopped to look at the sleeping boy, he noted the cylinder still strapped across his shoulder.

"This boy seems hardly the courier type," he mused.

On a premonition, he squatted beside the sleeping boy. Carefully he pulled the rolled message from the carrier. He held it to the light of the brilliant moon.

"Ah hah, as I expected! Foul play."

The message read:

Put this boy to death immediately.
If he arrives by day, kill him by day.
If he arrives by night, kill him by night.

Cautiously the ascetic took a pen from under his tunic. He changed the message, rerolled the scroll and slipped it back into the cylinder.

When the boy awakened the next day, he suspected nothing. He resumed his mission.

When he reached his destination, he was met by a guard. The young man gave the cylinder to him to deliver to the evil queen's daughter.

The lovely daughter read the message.

It read:

Treat this man well. Give him your heart.
If he arrives by day, marry him by day.
If he arrives by night, marry him by night.

Being obedient as daughters are meant to be, she proceeded to carry out her mother's wishes.

After the ceremony, the lovely young wife showed her husband all the spacious rooms of the fine palace. That is, all except one.

"You would hide something from your husband?" he teased.

"It is not mine to show you. Please do not tempt me to disobey my mother."

Driven by curiosity, the young man waited until his wife was fast asleep. Then he took the key and ran with haste to the forbidden room.

The key fit the door perfectly. It turned with ease. The door flew open.

The young man peered in. The room was empty except for a long shelf running the length of the far wall. The husband scanned the single shelf in the dim light cast from the open doorway.

He stepped into the forbidden room. Again, he surveyed the walls, corners, and the long shelf. His vision adjusted to the darkness. Then he gasped. Staring hauntingly at him was the jar of twenty-four sad eyes.

Wasting no time, he grabbed the jar, hid it under his sarong and fled from the palace.

Now inside the palace, the young wife stirred. She reached out to her new husband. Abruptly she awakened when she realized his mat was empty.

She was on her feet in an instant.

She ran through the great corridors calling him. Then she saw the open door of the secret room.

She called for the guards. They called the grand army. All set out in pursuit.

The fleeing husband heard the thunderous approach of the army. He had to outwit them so he could aid his imprisoned mother and her eleven sisters.

The young wife, held by obedience to her parent, stood by crying for her love. She wailed so forlornly that, in time, she collapsed from a broken heart. Where she fell, it is said her body was transformed into the majestic, rolling Neang Kangrei mountains that border our Kompong Chhang Province."

"See them some day, Jaya. You'll understand what I believe the story means." And the two sat alone, each with his own thoughts.

Finally Laksmei spoke up again. "You asked me why I feel I must stay with my brother even when I don't want to. Neang Kangrei's young husband knew. And I know too. There is an order to things. Destroy that order and it will one day destroy you. Blood lines must not be broken. The young man had a mother and eleven aunts to care for. I have no mother, but I do have a brother."

She laid her hand lightly on Jaya's strong, young arm. Then she vanished back into the blackness of the night.

VI

The sun rose, and with its predictable rising, the dank, unbreathable heat dazed them just as did the silence left by the runaways.

No one spoke. There was no reason to speak. Betrayal and loyalty. Both achieved the same end. The parting of ways. Three, because they wanted to. One, because she was compelled to.

As though by force of habit, Hiran and Prithivin and Jaya went about the business of living out the season of illness and the season of recovery. Each was often alone with his thoughts. Yet all were bound together by need.

And thus came the time for another parting.

"You have become master of the line and shaft," Hiran told Prithivin one day while they sat eating the lad's morning catch. "For a village boy, you have become a fine fisherman and hunter. You have grown cautious and cunning and have developed the qualities of a man of strategy. I suggest that you seek out men of military ability. Ally yourself with the great maharajas. Learn from them."

Then Hiran turned to Jaya. Quietly he said, "You, my son, knew the lessons of caution and cunning. To them you have added endurance. But your greatest learning is yet to come." He laid his hand on the boy's shoulder.

"I charge you to travel south to the great courts of the Sailendra kingdom in Java. Seek out the kingdom's wisest man. Tell him that the Brahman Hiranyadama sent you. He will understand."

"As for myself, I have been awarded restored health, a gift from the great god Siva. You, Jaya, have been his agent of healing. I will continue my pursuit of life's meaning."

The three stood silent for a moment, encircled by the strong ties of deep affection and mutual respect. The two young men bowed deeply to the kindly Hiran. Then they watched as he turned from them and went his plodding, determined way.

The thick forest took him from them. Soon they could no longer hear the muffled dragging of the crippled leg.

Jaya and Prithivin turned to each other. With the intensity of two strong, young tiger cubs, they flung themselves into each other's arms. Then, releasing their hold, parted without looking back.

Prithivin, in a full run, struck out in the direction of the setting sun, failing to look back in time to see his friend make his move that would change both their lives.

Jaya faced south.

VII

"Ah hah, the Brahman Hiranyadama knew his business well. Well, indeed," mused the Wise Man. "You have been in the courts of the mighty Sailendra three years — three important years, I must add. Now your apprenticeship here is over. It is well that you travel north again. Back to the lands of your youth. Back to your people."

"But why must I go? I enjoy life in the court. I'm making progress in the service of the king. I've only begun my training from the ministers and astrologers," Jaya protested. "As for my people, you know that I have none, my lord. I know only the jungles and rivers in the lands to the north."

"Such knowledge is valuable, my boy," replied the Wise One. And although you claim you are not of the lands to the north, consider this. You are not of this land, either."

Jaya fingered the talisman at his neck. "True, sir," he murmured.

"Come then. I will go with you. On our journey you will learn many valuable lessons. And when that journey is over, my son, your destiny will be clear to you."

Though the Wise Man's words disturbed Jaya, they also intrigued him. They were a mystery very much like the unexplained talisman that he always wore.

With deeply mixed feelings, the handsome young man of the mighty Javanese court set his sights northward.

"Here, give me your hand, my lord." Jaya reached down and helped the Wise One up onto the great elephant. "Quiet! Stand still there!" Jaya ordered the impatient beast.

This time, Jaya's travels began with an elegance unlike that of his long journey south, three years before. He and the Wise Man waved good-bye to the smartly dressed courtiers who had become his friends. Then Jaya turned the animal sharply to the north. "I don't like farewells," Jaya murmured.

Settled into the ornately carved elephant-chair saddle given them by their friends of Java's nobility, Jaya called over his shoulder, "May we meet again." Then they set off on their rocking, swaying way to the fringe of the mighty Sailendra kingdom.

From there, they traveled north to the sea. When they arrived they traded the great elephant for a sturdy boat and some able seamen.

Jaya studied the seamen. He noted the way they clutched their toes about the gunwales and pushed forward with a peculiar jerking stroke which is so characteristic of Cambodian river men. Learned, no doubt, from the earliest Khmers who dragged nets through fish-filled waters.

In time Jaya and his companion reached the tip of Malaysia. From there they traveled by land up the Malay Peninsula, across what would one day become Thailand and Laos. Then along the great Mekong river to the heart of the land.

One day, Jaya awakened elated. Dawn streaked the sky with tiger stripes. The air was clear and hot.

"Wise One," Jaya called. "Come up on the side of the hill. See how the country resembles a shallow dish. Look at that range of hills over there," he pointed. The ones the villagers tell us are the Cardamon mountains. And the Elephant mountains stretching beyond them. They curve like the rim of a vast saucer."

The Wise One looked where Jaya pointed. He listened to his description with satisfaction.

Back in their crude camp, they gathered their few things — knife, pot, mats, and they set out once more. They continued to follow the great river, gathering berries along the shore. Occasionally they stopped to lower their small nets for a fish or two. Lily beds seemed to come alive in the quivering heat waves at the water's edge. From under banyan trees, naked fishermen stood watching them furtively. Wild water buffalo grazed in black clumps.

At times Jaya spotted elephant tracks in the marshy shore. They heard them wild and free, crashing through dry bamboo at their play. Jaya recalled his days in the jungles where the elephant and especially the tiger were the undisputed overlords.

Traveling south, Jaya saw how the great Mekong and its countless finger-like tributaries played a crucial role in the life of the people. These streams provided water for rice fields. They gave shelter to billions of fish.

But what he saw of the greatest of Mekong's tributaries, the river Tonle Sap, distressed him.

"Look, Wise One, how mysteriously this river appears to change its direction twice a year!"

Jaya spoke to half-naked men and women who stood knee deep in rice paddy fields. They told him how they could only harvest rice when the tributaries were full. When Tonle Sap was swollen, the fishing was unsurpassed.

But when the dry season set in, black, stagnant pools formed. Green scum covered them. Swarms of insects hovered everywhere.

Leaving the river Jaya and the Wise Man turned inland. A villager or occasional traveler told them what they knew about local trails, wayside temples and rest stations. Jaya and the old man fought their ways along. The rutted paths were nearly hidden by the close-grown thickets of scrub forest. Blinded with sweat they tripped over tangles of roots and trailing rattan vines. Dusty snake grass beat across their faces. Cobras slipped silently across the path, paused long enough to swell their hoods, then slithered on. Conversation was muffled in spurts of choking dust. Birds that huddled on the trail took off in drowsy flight as they heard them approach.

"The temple! Up ahead! I think that is it," Jaya called.

Half hidden in the labyrinth of trees, a small green-brown temple spilled its tiles through webs of vines and giant banyan roots.

Jaya and the Wise One fought their way to it. Dank, moist coolness welcomed them as they stepped up on its pavilion. They sat down on its moss-covered steps, wiped the sweat from their faces and brushed away the insects that droned across the shafts of light where the sun pierced the shady green.

"We made our destination none too soon, son," the Wise One told Jaya. "When the monsoon arrives there will be no travel. I suggest we wait out this rainy season here."

Scarcely had they settled in than the rains began. Jaya and the Wise One sat cross-legged on the temple's stone floor. Drops spattered on the ground around them. Rain gathered into little pools that filled and ran into each other. The tiny rivulets curved with maddening indecision here and there through the forest. They dallied around small mounds, turning back, veering sidewise, until it seemed they couldn't have come from anywhere nor would they ever lead any place.

Jaya marveled at the beauty around him. The stately Po trees with their broad leafy, protective arms. The Nakree with her heavy, fragrant blossoms. But he pondered most the poor people's plight. They lived part of the year in plenty when the rains fell and their world turned green and the rice grew tall. Then followed the months of near starvation when the waters receded. Dry, exposed soil turned hostile to tender growing plants. Jaya wondered too at the ruthless rulers who, like the monsoons, held the people in their powerful grip.

As though reading his thoughts, the Wise One spoke, "Jaya, we have seen the effects of power — the power of nature and the power of man. Stay here by me. Let the rain be the music. Your mind, the stage. I will provide the characters."

And the Wise One began this tale . . .

"In utter contentment — as though sitting down to a sumptuous meal spread on fine mats with delicate porcelain ware — a caterpillar one day sat himself down to the finest of caterpillar banquets. There before him lay a broad, green, tender young leaf of the Champa tree.

He wiggled himself comfortably into a niche in the tree bark and pulled the plump green leaf close to him. He looked it over well and in great anticipation. He drank deeply of a sweet dewdrop lying radiant on its broad surface. He pressed his cheek to its moist skin. He prepared to take the first delicious bite.

Suddenly, he was interrupted. An ominous shadow took form over the tree branch where he sat. The caterpillar shuddered.

Summoning what courage he could, he looked up timidly. A crow of awesome proportions hovered over him. Black, it glistened in the morning sun.

The caterpillar muttered, "I don't like the look in that crow's eyes. He has designs, and I have a strong feeling those designs concern me." Refusing to show his fright, however, the caterpillar began to nibble the tender leaf.

The caterpillar sensed the crow wasn't easily rebuffed. No doubt he was thinking, "Fortune is with me."

The crow sprang to a nearby limb. "Enjoy that bite, Caterpillar," he jeered. "The fatter you are, the better my morning meal."

Calling up what little courage he had left, the caterpillar tossed its tiny head. "Not so fast," he charged.

The crow blinked startled eyes. The caterpillar went on, "I have, Sir, this, to say to that." He cleared his throat, surprised at his own daring. "Since you are such a confident crow, then perhaps you can solve my riddle. In which case, if you answer correctly, your breakfast will be that much more enjoyable to you. But, if you cannot, you will find your meal elsewhere, of course."

"Can you be serious?" the crow smirked. "Oh, well, what's a little delay. Let's have the riddle. First we'll please the head. Then, the stomach."

The caterpillar nudged his leaf with deliberate care. He found an especially juicy spot. He took a large, round bite and chewed it slowly and satisfyingly.

"On with it!" crowed the bird, his mouth beginning to water.

"But, of course," agreed the caterpillar. He pursed his lips and blotted his mouth discretely against a dry edge of the leaf. "First," began the caterpillar, "you are to name the sweetest thing in all the world."

"The sweetest thing in all the world?" the crow repeated, looking somewhat disdainful.

"Next, you are to name the most bitter thing to be found."

The crow sighed.

60

Ignoring him, the caterpillar went on. "Then the most putrid, and finally, the most fragrant," and without a pause he added, "Please proceed."

The crow cleared his throat. He began his answers as though he solved riddles daily. "Anyone knows that sugar is the sweetest thing in the world. And honey," he added for good measure. "And there can be nothing more bitter than vinegar and lemons. The most putrid?" The crow rolled his eyes in boredom. "Everyone knows the stench of manure or decayed bodies answers that question." The crow pecked an imagined fleck of dirt from his raven feathers. "As for the most fragrant, well, that is most naturally the beautiful blooms of the Champa tree. They are the most fragrant." The crow's voice trailed off confidently.

"Have you finished?" the caterpillar asked politely.

"Finished?" squawked the crow. "Of course, I'm finished. And now may I begin."

"Not so fast." The caterpillar stood his ground. "The contest is not over. The riddle is not solved. Your answers, you see, just happen to be wrong, wrong, wrong, and wrong again."

The crow swallowed hard. "Wrong?"

"Wrong," said the caterpillar emphatically.

"You are telling me that the answers I have given you are not right?"

"I would say that this is the only time this morning that you have been correct."

"What?"

"Precisely. Note the right answers."

The crow cawed his disdain.

"Not so fast," cautioned the caterpillar. "First, remember our bargain."

"Yes. Yes," spat the crow impatiently. "On with the answers."

"I am frankly astonished," began the caterpillar, "that you did not know that loving words uttered in sincerity are the sweetest thing in all the world. Nor, for that matter, do I understand why you did not know that hurtful, wounding words flung about unjustly are the most bitter things. And the most putrid — an evil reputation, a bad name among men. As for the most fragrant, a good name among men, a reputation for integrity, honesty and kindness."

The crow tucked his head under his wing in shame.

As for the caterpillar, he turned back to his tender leaf and resumed his nibbling, contentedly."

Both the Wise One and Jaya chuckled lightly at the tale. Then Jaya spoke, "What you tell in that fable is what perplexes me most. The crows of the world so unfeelingly devour the caterpillars of the world. The powerful consume the humble to their own ends." Jaya's brow furrowed.

"And," added the Wise One, "in so doing, well-springs of wisdom are destroyed. What, therefore, do you learn about earthly power and of wisdom?

"From what I have seen, worldly power without wisdom is brutish and cruel. I have seen whole kingdoms of people controlled by a powerful few. And to do so," he added, "the majority are made to fear the few. People, bent low in the rice fields, fearing the whims of nature and the threat of starvation. People cringing before tyrants, fearing their every whim and fancy. Their dreams crushed and their hopes for a better life dried up like the shrunken, cracked earth under the harsh tropical sun.

Jaya sat, his head in his hands. The old man said no more but dozed fitfully beside him, claiming whatever rest he could, as though he somehow knew what was about to happen.

VIII

"Hello. Hello!" Up the path toward the temple, a man came running. His voice was tinged with urgency. Slipping and sliding, he made his way through the mud and slime. "Hello," he called again. When he reached the steps of the temple, he kicked off his muddy sandals. "Is anyone here?" He sat down on one of the steps. He washed his feet hurriedly in one of the puddles. Then he dried them on a cloth that he took from a sack slung over his shoulder. Quickly, he stood to his feet. Although he was grimy from travel during the wet season, the fabric of his sarong didn't hide the fact that he appeared to be a man of means. Strongly built, perhaps in his middle years, he crept reverently to the door of the temple. He peered in. The Wise One was seated in meditation.

"Oh, kind Sir," he blurted. "If your humble servant may be so bold as to disturb you."

The wise old man looked into the desperate face of the man before him. "Yes?" he responded.

"Could it be that you are the Wise One from the courts of Sailendra? If you are, I have been hunting you for weeks."

"You must be very tired," the old man said sympathetically.

"Not too tired to seek audience with the Wise One."

"The season of rains is nearing its end. The day is well spent. If you have been searching for me for weeks, then one more night cannot matter in the whole scheme of time. Come, my friend, rest yourself. Eat with me and tomorrow we will speak of your mission."

The man fell to his knees before the Wise One. He stammered his gratitude at having finally found him. But he was persistent. "Please, my lord, hear me out. I come not for myself alone, but for my people."

"If your mission cannot wait until tomorrow at least let it wait until you have eaten," the Wise One advised.

Jaya, seeing that the old man was much involved with the visitor, remained hidden in the inner rooms of the temple.

Later that night after he had unrolled his mat and prepared to sleep, Jaya heard the shuffling footsteps of the old man approaching his quarters.

"Jaya, my boy, are you awake?" His whisper had grown hoarse with age.

Jaya was instantly alert. "Yes, Sir. I am awake. Do you need help?"

"Come with me," he beckoned. With labored steps, he walked slowly along the long corridor that led past Jaya's quarters to his own.

Jaya rubbed his eyes and jumped to his feet. He hurried to follow the old man.

The arc of light from the coconut oil lamp moved falteringly along the uneven stone walls of the gallery.

When they reached the old man's quarters, the Wise One turned to Jaya, "Please, my boy, take this lamp and help me to my mat."

Jaya took the oil lamp from his hand and set it on the floor. Then he put his arm around the old man and eased him down gently.

"There are things we should consider, Jaya. Tonight is as good a time as any to do so."

Jaya took a cotton wrap from a stool nearby. He put it around the shoulders of the old man, noting as he did so how frail the old one had grown during the rainy months. Then Jaya sat down cross-legged before him.

"You saw the visitor who came here today?" he asked "You heard the import of his mission?"

"I saw him, yes, my lord. But I did not hear what he said. It seemed that he was in need of your private audience. I stayed in the far rooms of the temple."

"Then you did not hear about whom he spoke?"

"No, Sir, I did not."

"I'm glad, because I prefer that you hear this from me. Our visitor claims his name is Sulayman, a prosperous merchant by trade. His business has taken him throughout this land and, by ship, to the lands beyond.

According to Sulayman while you and I have been on our journey concerned about our own affairs, grievous things have been taking place. Wherever we have traveled, we have managed to miss hearing the worst. With the onset of the monsoons, we hid away here from the strife of the world."

"You are troubled, Wise One?" Jaya asked.

"Troubled, yes. I am always troubled when I learn of violence and injustice. And yet, as a storm can only roil the sea's surface, the quiet spirit of the deep remains. My soul knows that we near the end of such tumultuous times."

66

Jaya's eyes were wide with foreboding.

"Listen closely, my son.

It seems that while the fortunes of this land have risen and fallen under a succession of kings, some, as you and I have observed, have been wise and prudent. Others, weak and ineffectual. Meanwhile, neighboring states have constantly threatened this land. Not all have been successful. One king has been particularly unsuccessful. He was not esteemed by his subjects because he was reckless and impetuous. He is known to have displayed no compassion for his people. Instead, he concentrated privilege on the nobility alone. His oppressive rule has resulted, according to Sulayman, in widespread civil unrest.

Sulayman tells that one day after discussing the affairs of state with his Chief Minister, the young king began complaining bitterly about his fortune. He blamed this person and that, this group and another. Then his tirade took a dangerous turn. He began speaking enviously of the Kingdom of Zabag."

"Zabag?" Jaya exclaimed, his mouth dropping open.

"Yes, Jaya. The Maharaja of Zabag whom you and I know as Sailendra. But let me continue.

The merchant Sulayman went to great lengths to describe the Maharaja's realm. He said it contained much of Sumatra, Java, and Malaysia. Then, he dwelled long on the single feature that made Sailendra's reign so noteworthy — his large fleet of tough, fast-moving vessels manned by fearless, disciplined crewmen.

It seems that the young Cambodian king in his outrageous display, turned suddenly to his Chief Minister and shouted, 'I have only one desire and that is to see on a tray before me the head of the Maharaja of Zabag!'

The Chief Minister was shocked and perplexed. A ruler as powerful as the great Maharaja was sure to have spies within the Cambodian court.

The Minister glanced about him to assure himself that he and the young king were indeed alone. Then he said, 'I implore you, Your Majesty, never express such a wild wish. Should it be overheard, the consequences could be grave.'

But Sulayman told me the young king, Mahipativarman, would not be quieted.

'Please,' begged the Minister. 'The people of Zabag and those of our kingdom have enjoyed only the best of relations. We must be careful to preserve harmony between our states.'

But the Minister's advice served only to enrage the king further. So, at a court function, the boastful young monarch repeated his wish.

A hush fell over everyone. Terror filled the hall.

Now what the Chief Minister feared, came true. The boast did fall on disloyal ears. It filtered to the Maharaja who, at first report, could not believe what he had been told. So he dispatched a trusted officer to verify it. When confirmation was received, the Maharaja called a secret session. Sailendra vowed to punish the impudent king.

A plan was laid. First, he swore his council to secrecy. Then he ordered one thousand ships to cruise the waters bordering Cambodia and sail about casually, inconspicuously. At an appointed time, they were to rendezvous, sail to the mouth of the river and advance on the Cambodian capitol in a surprise attack.

'One condition', Sailendra is supposed to have told his men, 'spare the people's lives. Tell them they need not flee. It is only the king that I want. It is with him and him alone that I have business.'

After a few days, the fleet met as arranged. It sailed to the mouth of the river, advanced on the capitol and captured it with ease.

The Maharaja went directly to the evacuated palace. He seated himself on the sovereign's throne. There, he waited for the hapless young king to be brought before him.

When this was accomplished, the Maharaja demanded, 'Why have you expressed such a foolish wish? What has my kingdom done that you wish the Maharaja of Zabag dead?'

The young king stood before him chagrinned and speechless.

The Maharaja went on. 'It is good for you that you did not say you would seize my kingdom and ravage my land as well. Thus I will deal with only what you actually said. Your punishment will be what you wished for me.'

Everyone gasped.

'I will return to my people without the spoils I'm entitled to. This will serve as a lesson to others who may be tempted to speak as rashly as you.'

With that the Maharaja signaled his executioners. They forced the bewildered young king to his knees and lopped off his head.

Then the Maharaja turned to the trembling old Minister and praised him for what he was told was the Minister's wise council to the unruly young king.

The Maharaja lost no time sailing back home with the head of the young monarch.

Later, he returned the head to the Cambodians as a warning to future braggarts.

Jaya could scarcely believe what he heard. He recalled his life in the Sailendra court. He recalled the lessons he had learned from the ministers and astrologers.

But this. This was hideous beyond belief.

Stunned, Jaya asked, "Can this be so?"

"Although you protested when I urged you to leave the courts of Sailendra, I knew that the time had come when we would have had no choice but to leave.

The months given to your journey north were what they were meant to be. It is obvious that Sailendra has grown more powerful. The extent of his ambition is, of course, only a guess."

Jaya sat entranced.

"Two things stand out boldly, my son. Since this dastardly act, the people of this land have been subjected to a succession of tyrants, some foreign. Whichever, one was no worse than the one he succeeded."

"But Sailendra?" Jaya stammered, still unbelieving.

"Keep this one thing in your mind above all others. Sailendra would say he acted justly. He meted out one evil for another. But justice alone, my son, when it is un-

69

tempered by compassion, is little better than injustice. Let me explain it this way," and the Wise One began . . .

"A girl's parents watched a young man make his way up their path one day.

"Ah hah," said the father.

"Umm," said the mother.

The young man climbed the steps of the house that sat high on sturdy stilts. Walking around to the veranda where they sat, he raised his hands together in the formal greeting used by all Cambodians. He bowed slightly to show his respect.

The father and the mother nodded in response.

"My lord," began the young man, addressing the father, "I am very much in love with your daughter. Will you grant her hand to me in marriage?"

"Oh?" said the father.

"Umm," said the mother.

The young man launched into a finely prepared speech calculated to impress the parents with his honorable intentions.

"Words have an easy way about them," said the father.

"Uh huh," agreed the mother.

"It is not until intentions are translated into actions that their quality can be judged," the father said.

"Ah hem," the mother agreed.

"I stand prepared to prove my love," the young man answered eagerly.

"Then we will take you at your word," the father told him.

But the father was in no hurry for his only daughter to marry. Her springlike beauty graced his golden years.

Nor was the mother eager to see her daughter leave for she brewed a heady pot of tea.

So the two excused themselves and considered the matter in private.

When they returned, the young man affirmed, "I will meet any request."

"So be it," said the father.

The mother sat with her hands folded in her lap.

"You will want to prove your endurance and your fortitude, I am sure," said the father.

"By all means," replied the young suitor.

"This then will be your test. You will have your arms and legs bound tightly. Then, you will be submerged up to your neck in the nearby lake. You are to maintain that position for three days and three nights. However cold you become, you must not in any way move to warm yourself."

The young man swallowed with difficulty. What choice did he have? He had already agreed to the test. So, he took his leave and went away somewhat less brightly than he came.

Now the parents could see the lake clearly from their thatch-roofed home. They checked on the suitor periodically.

The first day passed uneventfully. As did the first night.

Then the second day.

And the second night.

On the third day, the parents seldom left the veranda, so constantly did they watch the young man.

By the third and final night, the father and mother literally hung over the railing watching for the slightest move.

Suddenly a light on the far shore distracted them. They observed it closely and decided it was a briskly burning bonfire.

The daughter herself watched with growing interest, peering from behind the door.

"Ah hah!" the father exclaimed suddenly. "The test is over. Pull him out."

The young man had turned his head ever so slightly, obviously interested in the activity on the far shore as the others were.

"We won!" the father said, triumphantly.

And the mother returned to her seat on the veranda and folded her hands in her lap.

"It was hideously unfair," the suitor complained to the magistrate the next day.

The magistrate informed him that he could arrive at no ruling unless the parents were also present.

So the parents were requested to appear. When they arrived they greeted the magistrate cordially and presented him with a lovely gift.

The young man had been so distraught he had neglected this amenity.

This, the magistrate took into consideration.

Thanking the parents graciously for the gift, he finally ruled in their favor.

As if this were not enough, the magistrate turned to the young man and declared, "Not only have you failed the test and forfeited your right to marry the daughter, you must recompense the defendants by preparing and serving them a fine meal."

Little puffs of gray dust clouded around his feet with each dragging step the dejected young man took.

"Things are not so well with you, my son?"

The young man was startled out of his reverie. He looked in the direction of the voice. There, to the side of the dusty path, sat the most revered of Cambodia's wise and friendly animals, Honorable Rabbit.

The young man paused, then sat down by the rabbit. Sorrowfully, he poured out his unhappy tale.

When he finished, the rabbit said brightly, "I have an idea. Listen closely to what I tell you. You and I will set this matter straight."

The rabbit leaned close and whispered in the young man's ear. "Prepare a fine banquet. But do so with one condition. When you prepare the soup, leave out the salt. Instead, place the salt in a separate dish. Come now. Cheer up. I will go with you."

The young man followed the Honorable Rabbit's instructions carefully.

When the magistrate saw the young man coming up the path with the rabbit, he was careful to greet them both cordially. No matter what a man's rank, everyone regarded the Honorable Rabbit with respect.

"How glad I am to see you, Sir Rabbit," greeted the magistrate. "And what is the reason for this kind visit?"

The rabbit spoke right up. "I've come to help you with this case."

"But, the case is already closed, Honorable Sir. Do us the honor, nevertheless, to eat with us."

Everyone gathered around the mat laid before them — the magistrate, the two parents and the Honorable Rabbit.

The young man spread a fine banquet before them. Then he stood by to be of further service.

The magistrate gestured for all to begin. After one spoonful of soup, he shook his head. "Young man, there is a slight problem here," he said. "Will you tell me why you have not salted the soup?"

The Honorable Rabbit spoke up for the young man. "Kind Magistrate, perhaps I can answer you." He blotted his whiskers politely. "As you assumed the small fire burning on top of a far away hill could give heat to this young man, so the salt, proportionately distant from the soup, must surely be adequate to flavor your food."

The magistrate began to sputter. Then he fell silent.

The parents hung their heads shamefully.

The magistrate reversed his judgement.

The young suitor was declared the winner. He ran from the room calling to the maiden. She stepped from her hiding place where she had waited for just such a response."

"You see, Jaya," the Wise Man said, "Sailendra sought to achieve his end in his own way. To do so, he acted within the narrow limits of the law. In this case, a head for a head."

"So also in the case of the young man's trial by ordeal. The parents interpreted the young man's act so narrowly that while for their purposes, justice was served, all mercy and good sense were forgotten."

"With Sailendra, it is not his example of justice but his lack of mercy I would have you note. As the Honorable Rabbit implied, it is the intent of the heart, the seat of one's motives, which must, at all cost, be weighed."

At that, the Wise Old Man sighed deeply. "Please, my son, assist me as I lie down."

The strong young man took the small, fragile body into his arms. He laid him gently onto his mat. Then he picked up the oil lamp whose flickering light cast a mellow hue on the face of the weary man. Jaya saw in his serene, lined features the very qualities the sage sought to encourage in others. His lips relaxed into a faint smile.

For the first time, Jaya understood what the Wise One meant when he said that storms affect only the surface of life. Jaya knew that he was being priviledged to glimpse the eternal peace that lay beneath.

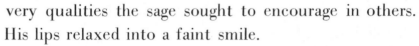

IX

The morning spewed forth like the steam from a boiling pot. The jungle shimmered and the rain-drenched landscape blurred in a hazy vapor.

"Come quickly, lad," the merchant Sulayman urged at the door of Jaya's quarters.

"Yes. Yes, my lord," Jaya answered.

"Haste! Woe to me and to my people," the man moaned as he led the way toward the old man's room. "The Wise One said to meet him this morning. He would advise me then. But I feared this. I feared something would happen."

Jaya followed, half skipping, half walking to keep up with the merchant Sulayman.

When the visitor reached the open doorway, he stopped and leaned heavily against its frame moaning pitiously. Jaya squeezed by him and pushed into the dark, stifling hot room. He stopped short. There, as though no time had passed between his bidding good night and his welcoming good day, lay the beloved old man, still and lifeless.

"He died before he could tell me what to do!" Sulayman cried in panic. "If nothing is done and my plot is exposed, the king will have his way again. He will do to me as he has done to everyone who has tried to rid our country of tyrants."

Sulayman began to sob.

Jaya went about his duties of a faithful son to a beloved father. While the despairing Sulayman filled the torrid air with wails, Jaya tenderly bathed the ancient body and clothed it in his finest tunic. Then he spread a pallet near the altar within the temple. He lifted the spent frame and carried it for the last time to the mat and to eternal rest.

Jaya summoned a youngster passing by the temple. He gave him a message and a few tokens as payment for its delivery. Then he sent him to the next temple with word for the priest to come and tend the body of the Wise Old Man. Only then, did Jaya turn to the grief stricken merchant.

"Why do you grieve so?" Jaya asked. "You have endured great hardship to reach the Wise One. You give up too easily, my lord. Surely to have become as successful a man as you are has meant facing discouragements of all kinds." Jaya was dismayed at his own reprimanding tone.

"But this has to do with life and death. This is no business venture," the merchant answered as he sat down on the steps on the temple, his shoulders slumped forward.

Jaya studied the man who had taken an enormous gamble. His livelihood was at stake. His very life was on the line. Jaya looked at Sulayman and suddenly felt a strange kinship with him. What he saw in the dispairing Sulayman was a whole nation, once prosperous and hopeful, now bent low by oppression.

X

Jaya, broad-shouldered, firmly built, stood in the center of the teeming market place. His sun-browned skin suggested a life lived close to nature. Around him he wore a loose skirt-like tunic, his powerful young chest and arms exposed. His black hair was pulled back from his forehead and wound casually in the top knot worn by the men of that day. His body glistened with the sweat of the endless summer.

He stood tall, solemn, scanning the clammoring crowd of people gathered around him.

He was unmistakably Cambodian with the rare combination of the stalwart Javanese to the south, and the fine aquiline features of the Indian to the west. And yet, for all that, there seemed something different about

Jaya, something that set him apart from the others. Perhaps it was his height for he stood a full head taller than most men. Perhaps it was the posture he assumed. An air of unconscious confidence. A hint of dignity. Or his eyes, sensitive yet compelling. Eyes that bore a hint of fierceness yet gentle with the suggestion of compassion.

Jaya smiled. His satisfaction spread like a brother's protective arm around the shoulders of his frightened young brothers and sisters. The people pressed closer to him.

Then, as though shaken by a tidal wave of heat, the white hot tropical air quivered momentarily, then erupted with shouts and cries. Men and women sank to their knees before him chanting praise and gratitude. Uplifted hands appealed to him. Bowed heads honored him. Old people, bent with years, stood silent, too overcome to cry out. Children clung to mothers' skirts, not knowing how to express their awkward wonder.

Jaya looked to the edge of the crowd where there had been a brief skirmish, now quieted. A resistance quelled by the strong figure of another young man. One Jaya had known from his youth. It was Prithivin who led captive this menacing foreign Maharaja. Here in the very market place where another Maharaja, the one called Sailendra, had displayed the head of the impetuous young Cambodian king.

Then Prithivin spotted Jaya. He turned the villainous tyrant over to the guards and dashed through the crowd to Jaya's side. As he drew near, Jaya bowed his head. "Thank you, faithful friend, for acting on my message. You have done a job for which thousands will call you great."

The once cocky Prithivin bowed low before his old friend. Then he lifted his eyes and spoke in low tones. "When I heard from you, I knew exactly what to do. My years with the warring Maharajas were well spent."

"As were mine at the courts of Sailendra," Jaya replied.

"Ah, but there is a difference," Prithivin countered. "While I learned the ways of brute battle, life against life, you learned the art of peace. Life for a life."

He moved closer to Jaya. "Are you prepared for what this means? These people will not stop short of declaring you their king."

"I'm aware of that," Jaya answered. "It gives me an uneasy feeling. You know who I wish were here right now?"

"Hiran," Prithivin replied without hesitation.

"Right."

"I happen to know where to find him!" Prithivin darted away through the crowd.

Jaya studied the throng of people before him. They were a beautiful people, skin tanned by the tropical sun, hair, straight and glistening, like strands of ebony silk. And yet, no face was familiar to him. Where was the merchant Sulayman? If anyone was to be honored, surely it should be he. He who had risked his life to escape from the ruthless Maharaja. He had run day and night fighting the lonely terror of travel during the monsoon season. It was he who searched for the Wise One, he who laid the scheme to unseat the ruling tyrant.

But Jaya stood alone even though amid the throng. Alone as he had been in the jungles, and in the temples at the feet of learned men. Alone as he made his way along dusty village paths, alone in Java's royal courts. Were it up to the company of grateful people around him, he would never again know solitude.

Without thinking Jaya reached for the talisman that still hung to a thin strip of reed around his neck. He fingered the ridges of the first letter, graceful and curving. Then the beginning of the second. . .

XI

"Ah, the blessings of Siva. Together again!" Hiran's body was twisted with age. His right leg was now almost as useless as his left. His ancient face was weather-worn, yet his eyes sparkled with the light of wisdom. "This time we're together not for the making of predictions but for fulfilling them," he cried exultantly.

Jaya had grown disciplined and learned at the feet of great men. But he was powerless to withhold his welling emotion as he sat alone once more with his old friends, Hiran and Prithivin.

For a moment, the three were silent. It was Hiran who spoke first. "You'll be needing a capable general, my lordship. Prithivin will be that man. As for the government, you will want to consider seriously the. . ."

"Hiran, my lord!" Jaya interrupted. "Your vision is obviously sharper than mine. These assumptions are making my head reel. I beg of you, slow down. Questions dart and soar in my mind like kites on a capricious wind." Jaya shook his head unbelievingly. "How am I to know that I am to assume the throne of this land? Certainly there are many men as qualified. . .no, more qualified, than I. Even Sulayman. But he made it plain that he is a merchant and must be about his business. And as for the royal line. . ." Jaya clutched at the talisman at his neck.

Hiran cleared his throat and settled back against a cushion. His disfigured legs resisted his attempt to draw them up to a cross-legged position. He made himself as comfortable as he could. "Look at the question this way, my son," he began. . .

"There were once four young men. Fine friends. Able students. They were returning from a far country where they had gone to seek an education.

The first student was remarkably talented in telling fortunes, probing deep into the future.

The second student was a fine archer. It was rumored that his arrow could fly so swiftly and so far that it could pierce the very sun itself.

The third student gained his renown for underwater endurance and the fourth student had mastered the art of rituals and incantations that could put life into a lifeless body.

Their journey home was treacherous and tiring. When they came upon a vast lake, they decided to rest for a time before continuing their journey.

While the four students rested the astrology student proposed a problem to wile away the time and add a note of pleasure to their trip. "I will make a prediction," he said. "If it comes true, we will see how each of you uses your learning to deal with the situation."

Everyone agreed enthusiastically.

So the astrologer began some fevered calculations. "Ah ha," he said when he had finished, "By the time tomorrow's sun has reached the point where it breathes its drying breath on the last clinging dew drop, a giant Garuda bird will flash across the sky.

"A Garuda bird?" his friends gasped. "Aren't there horrible tales about those birds? Unless we hide, he will surely snatch us away."

"You overlook one thing," said the astrologer. "Your fear for your own lives clouds the importance of the burden you will see in the claws of the Garuda."

"You and your predictions," grumbled the archer. "I thought we were going to relax for awhile."

Nevertheless the students agreed to the contest. They slept fitfully that night, however.

The next morning the students were aroused from their sleep by a frightening, screeching sound.

"There," the astrologer pointed out. "My predictions are accurate. See that black speck against the sun."

They watched the horrible creature as it swept above their heads carrying a strange burden in its terrible claws.

A maiden!

The astrologer grabbed his board and began rechecking his calculations.

The diver crept to the edge of the lake and stood poised.

The priest practiced his incantations.

And the archer lifted his cross-bow to his chest. With a cry of triumph, he let fly his arrow. It met its mark.

The Garuda spun crazily in the air. Its great wings fluttered wildly. Its talons opened and released the precious burden.

The maiden floated from the sky like an autumn leaf from a shaken tree. She fell helplessly into the water.

The diver's slim, strong body sliced the water. Deeper and deeper he went until the waters were murky black. He searched the depths for the maiden and finally caught her trailing gown. He swept her into his arms and with powerful leg strokes, rose to the surface of the lake. He lifted her beautiful face out of the water to the lifegiving air. But she did not breathe. Her lithesome body lay back limp and still in the diver's arms.

"She must not die," the diver shouted.

The priest closed his eyes and murmured his magic words. He turned about three times, raised his hands, and as he did so, the maiden's eyelids opened. She blinked, then drew a breath. The smile that spread across her lovely face promptly won the heart of each of the students.

The diver placed her on his own dry mat.

The astrologer brought her his dry cloak.

The archer brought her food.

The priest sat nearby, watching over her.

When it became evident that each of the students had fallen hopelessly in love with the maiden, matters became complicated when it was learned that the maiden loved each one in return.

Faced with this dilemma, the friends agreed that before they became enemies, they would return to their old teacher and let him mediate the problem.

So the four students fashioned a litter from reeds and vines. Gently they placed the maiden between them and set off to find their teacher once more.

After the old teacher heard each student out, he praised them for their performance.

"But, my sons. My sons," he scolded. "You lack the one thing that instills your knowledge with value."

The students sat before their instructor, shamed and silent.

"What you lack, my sons, is wisdom to know when and why to use your talents. Come. Show me how you positioned yourselves and acted in this situation."

The astrologer sat down first.

Then the archer.

Next, the diver.

And fourth, the priest.

The teacher spoke first to the astrologer. "My son, in the relationship to this maiden, you are as a father. One concerned with the whole of life. As an astrologer, you deal with earthly and heavenly phenomena. You are concerned with life in its largest sense."

Then he turned to the priest at the end of the line. "You, my son, trained as a priest and taught to revive the dead, are to this maiden as the mother. Giver of life. You may move next to the astrologer."

Then the teacher turned to the young archer. "You are as an elder brother. One who protects."

And finally the old teacher turned to the young man who had risked his life to save the maiden. "It is you, my son, who is best fit to be this maiden's husband. It is you who set aside your own safety for hers. You dared death itself to bring her to life."

And the young students bowed their heads before the wisdom of their great teacher."

"Jaya, my son," said Hiran. "You are as the diver in this tale. You, like he, have responded to a people in need. You have risked your life for them. Now embrace them. Embrace them as a protecting, providing husband would embrace his bride."

Jaya sat in silence for many moments. Finally he whispered, "There must be no images."

"No what, my son?"

"No images. No inscriptions."

"No inscriptions?"

"Nothing. Nothing boasting of vain glorious successes as so many have done who have ruled this land before me."

"But, Jaya," Prithivin interrupted.

Jaya went on. "All temples. All buildings are to be erected in honor of the god Siva. I will serve only as his agent. Do you understand? Only then will I assume the throne." Jaya's voice had a finality about it. "Good works, and good works alone, will stand as testimony to my memory."

And so it was that the reign of Jaya, the great Jayavarman II, began.

After traveling once again throughout the beautiful countryside of Cambodia, he selected as a site for his capitol, the flat, well-watered region. Together with master engineers, he devised an intricate system of irrigation and water storage. Magically, his people began to harvest a miracle — three to four crops of rice each year.

Free. His people were free from their bondage to the mightly Mekong and the whims of the Monsoons.

Together with Hiran, Jaya gave the people a new religion. From this, they gained a meaningful explanation and purpose for their lives.

As he became identified with the great protector, Siva, so his people identified with Jaya as their protector. Because Siva was a god who would tolerate no superiors, Jaya freed his people from the threat of control by powerful neighbors and hundreds of lesser gods.

With an abundance of rice, Jaya's country did not have to rely on trade for its propersity. With the assurance of enough to eat and safety from fear of conquest, Jaya's people had fewer demands on their lives. It was then that they turned to artistic pursuits.

Jaya introduced the concept of the temple mountain, their sacred buildings fashioned like delicate lotus buds set high on man-made earthen mounds. From this venture burst art, architecture, and sculpture that would boggle the minds of people for generations to come.

Jayavarman II.

Historians and archeologists acclaim him the first and greatest of all Khmer kings. His fifty-year rule laid the groundwork for a culture and civilization that would rival those of Egypt, Greece and Rome. It was Jaya who set the forces in motion that resulted in the magnificent Cambodian city called Angkor Thom. It was Jaya who foresaw what was to become a way of life so advanced for that time that scientists today stand in awe of the achievements of these people so long ago.

History tells us that Jaya took the throne in 802 and that his reign established a magnificence that was to last until 1431..

Then suddenly, strangely, history grows vague. Facts blur. The great city, as well as an entire six hundred year civilization mysteriously returned to the tropical jungle from which it came.

Exactly why, precisely how, is not known.

Possibly invasion. Perhaps internal corruption.

All that is positively known of that first and greatest of all Khmer kings and his remarkable kingdom is what was recently uncovered from the side of an ancient temple hidden for centuries by the tangles of roots. Like the unsolved mystery of the broken talisman Jaya always wore around his neck, the temple inscription simply states. . .

> the great Jayavarman II seated
> himself on the lions which ornament
> his throne; he imposed his commands
> over kings; he established his
> residence on Mount Mahandra, and
> with all, he had within him
> no pride

. . . and the fragment of another inscription that tells that the great Jayavarman II was . . .

> A lotus indeed.
> But a lotus without a stem.

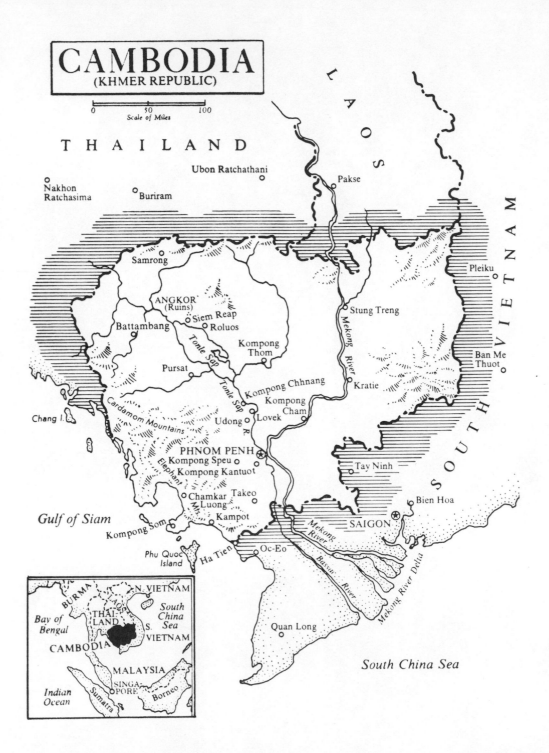

CAMBODIA
(KHMER REPUBLIC)

Scale of Miles
0   50   100

THAILAND

Nakhon
Ratchasima   Buriram   Ubon Ratchathani

LAOS

Pakse

Samrong

ANGKOR
(Ruins)
Battambang   Siem Reap
Roluos

Kompong
Thom

Pursat

Tonle Sap

Tonle Sap

Chang I.

Cardamom Mountains

Kompong Chhnang

Kompong
Cham

Udong
Lovek

R.

Stung Treng

Mekong River

Kratie

Pleiku

Ban Me
Thuot

SOUTH VIETNAM

PHNOM PENH
Kompong Speu
Kompong Kantuot

Elephant

Chamkar   Takeo
Luong
Kampot

Mts.

Gulf of Siam

Kompong Som

Phu Quoc
Island   Ha Tien   Oc-Eo

Tay Ninh

Bien Hoa

SAIGON

Mekong River

Bassac River

Mekong River Delta

Quan Long

South China Sea

BURMA   N. VIETNAM

LAOS

THAI-
LAND   South
China
Sea

Bay of
Bengal

CAMBODIA   S.
VIETNAM

MALAYSIA

Indian
Ocean   SINGA-
PORE

Sumatra   Borneo

A VERY BRIEF HISTORY
OF
CAMBODIA

Archaeological evidence indicates that the Khmer people have lived in the South East Asian peninsula since the Old Stone Age. They have left art objects, tools and implements, even towns and cities. It is assumed that this area was occupied from about 4000 B.C.

At the beginning of the Christian era, some small kingdoms coexisted along the middle and lower Mekong River. The first state was known as Founan and is thought to have been established by navigators and monks coming from India.

Between 560 and 630 approximately, Founan fell to its vassals and became known as Tchenla (or Kampudja).

Toward the end of the 7th century, Tchenla broke up making way for the Angkor period which spanned the 9th to 13th centuries.

In the year 802, Jayavarman II reestablished Khmer unity. He laid down the principles of sovereignty which were to be valid during the entire Angkorian period.

Jayavarman II declared independence from the influence of the Javanese Sailendras to the south and established a national religion that united king and god as one. It was during this 600 year period that the civilization grew to heights never again attained by the country.

After the 14th century, parts of the Khmer empire were taken away by Thai forces to the west and Annamese to the east. A dark period of fighting and surrender lasted for the next four centuries.

The French took over what was left of the Khmer empire as Cambodia in 1863. From that date until 1949 Cambodia was a French protectorate yet all the while retaining its own national identity.

In 1949 Cambodia was given self-rule within the French Union.

The country became a free state in 1954.

In 1970 Prince Sihanouk was stripped of his functions as Head of State and the Khmer Republic was established on October 9 of that year.

Since that time, however, Communists have taken over the country and its people. Thus Cambodia's doors, like those following the glory of the ancient Angkor period, closed, April, 1975.

ABOUT THE AUTHOR

Jewell Reinhart Coburn lived in the Far East where she taught both high school and college students. She traveled widely throughout the Orient and was herself a student of Asian ways.

When the South East Asian refugees arrived at California's Camp Pendleton, near her home, it was natural that she volunteer for the crash educational program established there.

From that encounter grew the friendships with Vietnamese and Cambodians that resulted in BEYOND THE EAST WIND: Legends and Folktales of Vietnam and KHMERS, TIGERS AND TALISMANS: From the History and Legends of Mysterious Cambodia.

ABOUT THE ILLUSTRATOR

Nena Grigorian Ullberg is a woman of rare sensitivity, with — as she says of herself — the soul of a gypsy. She came from Russia in her youth, and now lives in Southern California.

Nena's illustrations reveal a freedom of spirit a touch of whimsy, and a hint of poignancy. Nena has the distinction of being a great grandmother.